Flute Time Pieces 2

Compiled and edited by

Ian Denley

Contents

MUSIC DEPARTMENT

OXFORD
UNIVERSITY PRESS

OXFORD
UNIVERSITY PRESS

Great Clarendon Street, Oxford OX2 6DP, England
198 Madison Avenue, New York, NY10016, USA

Oxford University Press is a department of the University of Oxford.
It furthers the University's aim of excellence in research, scholarship,
and education by publishing worldwide

Oxford is a registered trade mark of Oxford University Press
in the UK and in certain other countries

1 3 5 7 9 10 8 6 4 2

ISBN 0–19–322106–3

Music and text origination by
Stave Origination
Printed in Great Britain on acid-free paper by
Caligraving Ltd., Thetford, Norfolk

Sonata in F, HWV369

1st and 2nd movements

George Frederick Handel
(1685–1759)

1. Larghetto ♩ = *c*.72

Printed in Great Britain

OXFORD UNIVERSITY PRESS, MUSIC DEPARTMENT, GREAT CLARENDON STREET, OXFORD OX2 6DP

Jo 12/1/09.

2. Allegro ♩ = 92+

Theme and Variation 3
from Introduction, Theme and Variations, D802

Franz Schubert
(1797–1828)

THEME

Sonata in D, W129
3rd movement

Carl Philipp Emanuel Bach
(1714–88)

Vivace ♪ = *c.*144
Dynamics should be chosen by the performers

Scherzino, Op. 55, No. 6

Joachim Andersen
(1847–1909)

lesto   agile, nimble-fingered
mobile   easy-moving

Sonatina in G, B183
2nd movement

Antonín Dvořák
(1841–1904)

Allegretto and Idylle

from Suite, Op.116

Benjamin Godard
(1849–95)

ALLEGRETTO

IDYLLE

Serenade

Albert Woodall

Dedicated to Louis Fleury

Syrinx

for unaccompanied flute

Claude Debussy
(1862–1918)

au mouvement	resume (the first) tempo	*retenu*	held back
cédez	slow down	*très modéré*	at a very moderate speed
en retenant jusqu'à la fin	slow down to the end	*très retenu*	very held back
marqué	marked, conspicuously	*un peu mouvementé (mais très peu)*	a little quicker (but very little)

* The fingering Th. O ● ● ● / ● ● ● C♯ gives an attractive colour to this D♭, but turn in a little to avoid sharpness.

Elegy, Op.142

Anthony Hedges
(b. 1931)

Andante Pastoral
Prelude

Paul Taffanel
(1844–1908)

Flute Time Pieces 2

Piano accompaniment book

Compiled and edited by

Ian Denley

Contents

MUSIC DEPARTMENT

OXFORD
UNIVERSITY PRESS

Sonata in F, HWV369

1st and 2nd movements

George Frederick Handel
(1685–1759)

Printed in Great Britain

OXFORD UNIVERSITY PRESS, MUSIC DEPARTMENT, GREAT CLARENDON STREET, OXFORD OX2 6DP

4

2. Allegro ♩ = 92+

Theme and Variation 3

from Introduction, Theme and Variations, D802

Franz Schubert
(1797–1828)

THEME

VARIATION 3

Sonata in D, W129

3rd movement

Carl Philipp Emanuel Bach
(1714–88)

Vivace ♪ = *c*.144

Dynamics should be chosen by the performers

Scherzino, Op. 55, No. 6

Joachim Andersen
(1847–1909)

Sonatina in G, B183
2nd movement

Antonín Dvořák
(1841–1904)

Poco più mosso

quasi spiccato

Allegretto and Idylle

from Suite, Op.116

Benjamin Godard
(1849–95)

ALLEGRETTO

IDYLLE

Quasi adagio, molto tranquillo ♩ = *c.*60

Serenade

Albert Woodall

Elegy, Op.142

Anthony Hedges
(b. 1931)

rit.   poco più mosso

Andante Pastoral

Prelude

Paul Taffanel
(1844–1908)